Shhh! Little Mouse

VIKING

Published by the Penguin Group
Penguin Group (Australia)
250 Camberwell Road
Camberwell, Victoria 3124, Australia
(a division of Pearson Australia Group Pty Ltd)
Penguin Group (USA) Inc.
375 Hudson Street, New York, New York 10014, USA
Penguin Group (Canada)
90 Eglinton Avenue East, Suite 700,
Toronto ON M4P 2Y3, Canada
(a division of Pearson Penguin Canada Inc.)
Penguin Books Ltd
80 Strand, London WC2R 0RL, England
Penguin Ireland
25 St Stephen's Green, Dublin 2, Ireland
(a division of Penguin Books Ltd)
Penguin Books India Pvt Ltd
11, Community Centre, Panchsheel Park, New Delhi -110 017, India
Penguin Group (NZ)
67 Apollo Drive, Mairangi Bay, Auckland 1310, New Zealand
(a division of Pearson New Zealand Ltd)
Penguin Books (South Africa) (Pty) Ltd
24 Sturdee Avenue, Rosebank, Johannesburg 2196, South Africa

Penguin Books Ltd, Registered Offices: 80 Strand, London WC2R 0RL, England

First published by Penguin Group (Australia), a division of Pearson Australia Group Pty Ltd, 2007

10 9 8 7 6 5 4 3 2 1

Designed by Deborah Brash © Penguin Group (Australia)
Typeset in 28pt Apollo
Printed and bound by Imago Productions, China

National Library of Australia
Cataloguing-in-Publication data:

  Allen, Pamela.
  Shhh! Little mouse

  ISBN-13: 978 0 670 07068 8
  ISBN-10: 0 670 07068 8

  I. Title.

A823.3

www.puffin.com.au

Shhh! Little Mouse

Pamela Allen

PENGUIN|VIKING

For Liam Robert

A little grey mouse
lives in our house.

See him peeping,
now tip-toe creeping.
Shhh! little mouse.

Who is that sleeping?

Shhh!

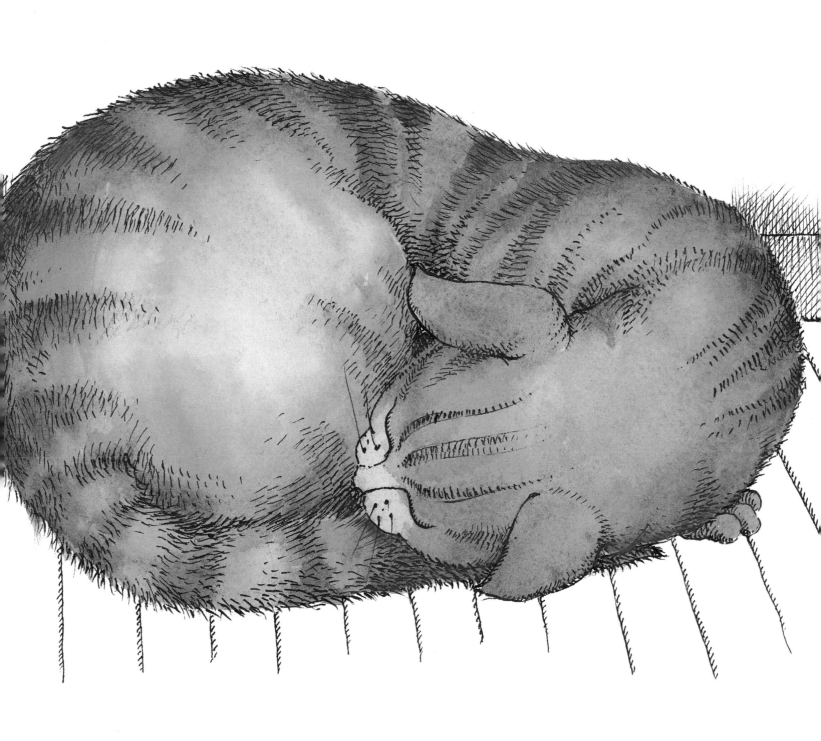

Peering, peeking, tip-toe creeping.
Shhh! little mouse.

What are you seeking?

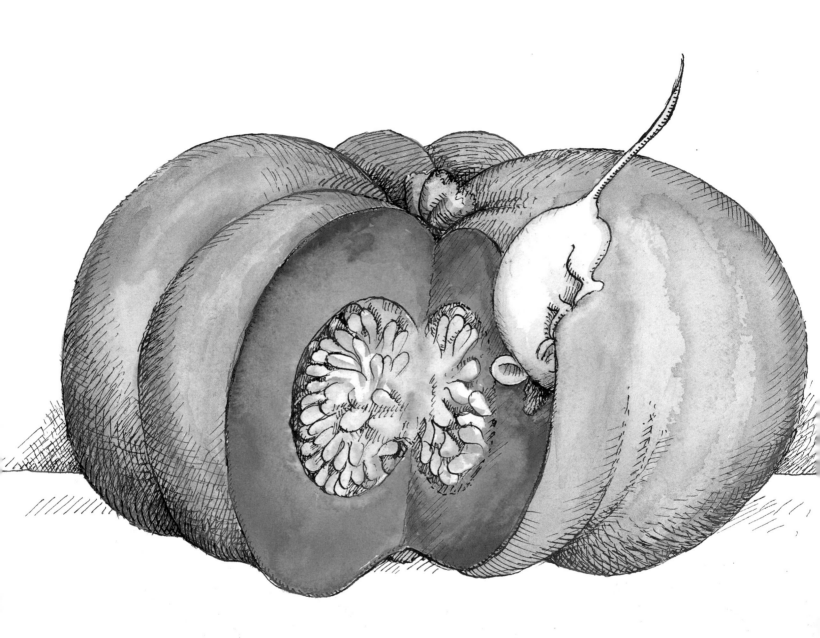

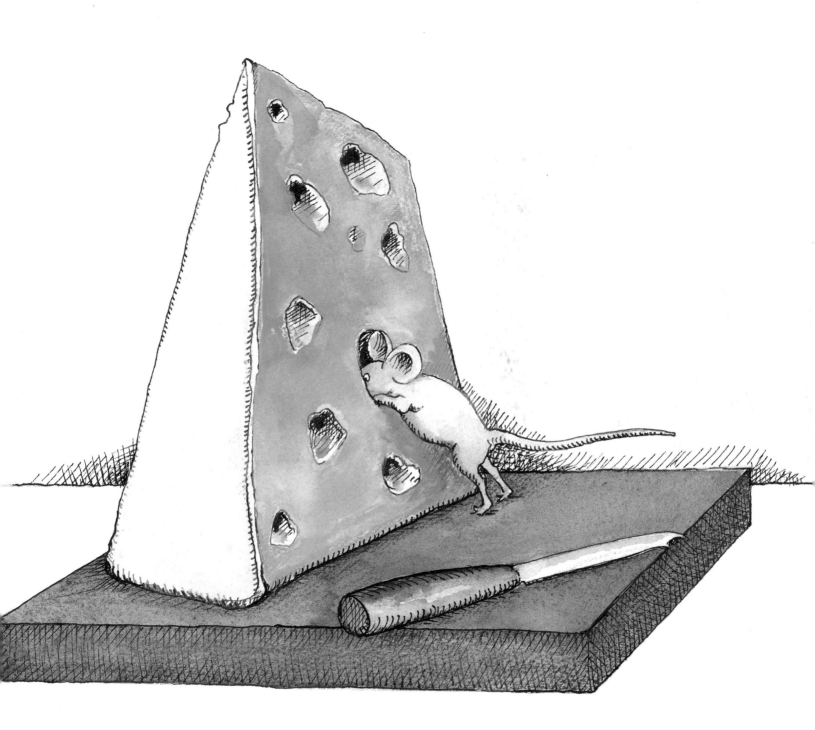

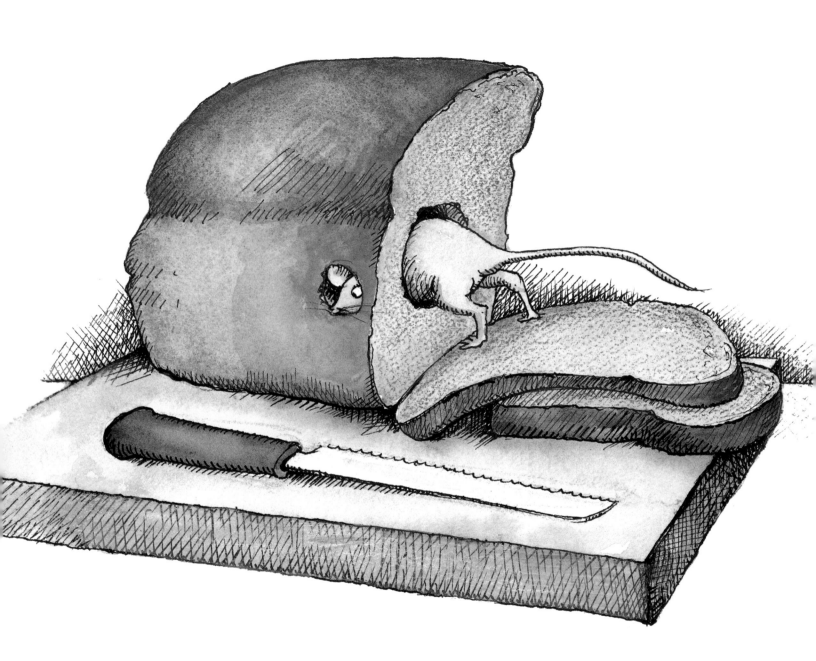

Careful, little mouse!

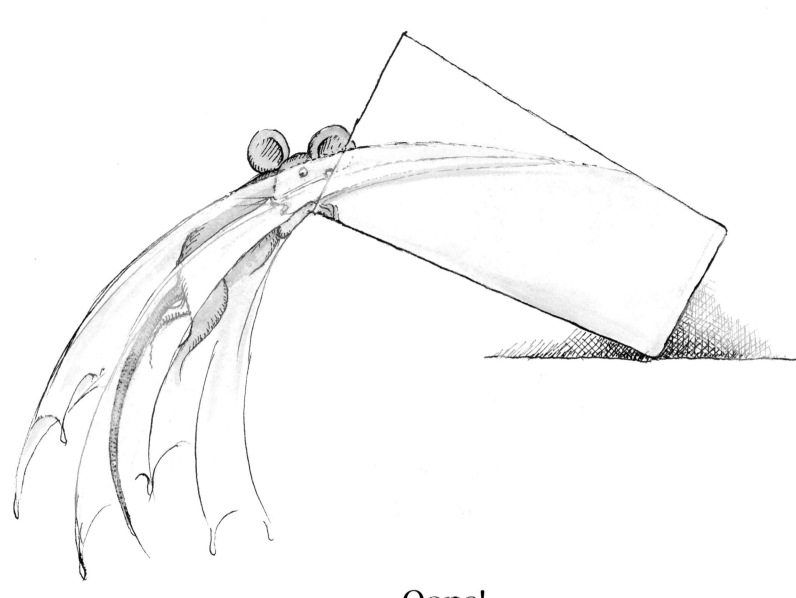

Oops!

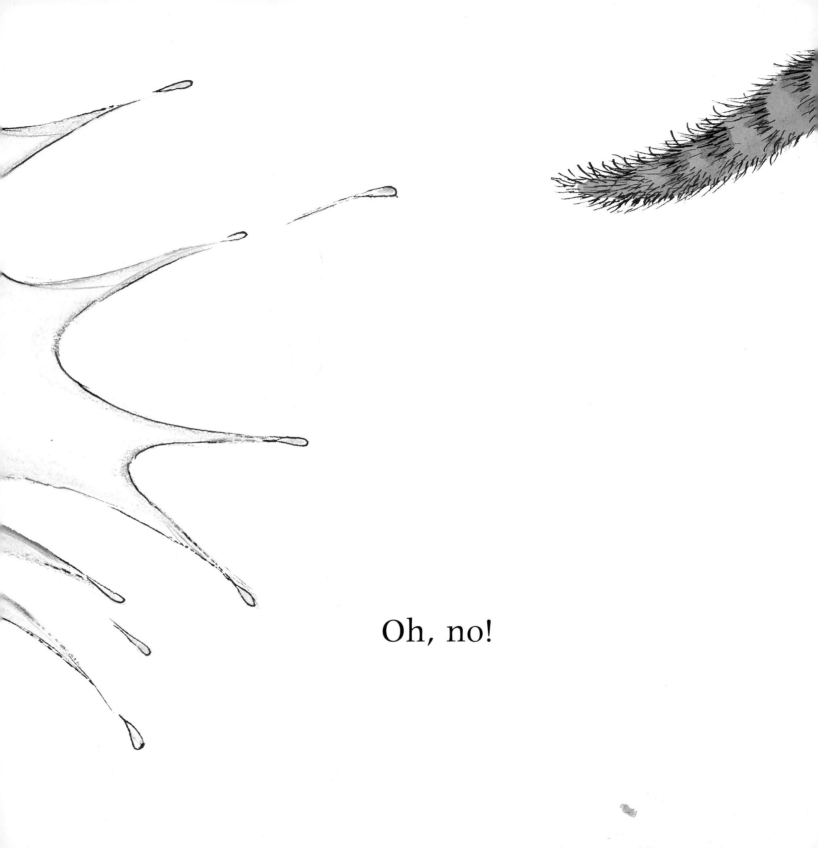

Oh, no!

Quick, little mouse.
Run, little mouse.

Run! Run! Run!

Good night, little mouse.